DJUSD
Public Schools
Library Protection Act 1998

A Day With A
Troubadour

A Day with a
Troubadour

by Régine Pernoud

Illustrations by Giorgio Bacchin
Translated by Dominique Clift

RP

Runestone Press/Minneapolis
A Division of the Lerner Publishing Group

All words that appear in **bold** are explained in the glossary that starts on page 43.

This edition first published in the United States in 1997 by Runestone Press.

Runestone Press, c/o The Lerner Publishing Group
241 First Avenue North, Minneapolis, MN 55401 U.S.A.

Photo are used courtesy of Zodiaque, p. 1; Xurxo Lobato, Santiago, pp. 8–9, 12 (top); Jurgen Richter, Pullach, p. 12 (bottom).

Library of Congress Cataloging-in-Publication Data

Pernoud, Régine.
[Un trovatore. English]
A day with a troubadour / by Régine Pernoud; illustrations by Giorgio Bacchin; translated by Dominique Clift.
p. cm. — (A day with—)
Includes biographical references and index.
Summary: Presents factual information about the lyric poets of medieval Europe as well as a fictional account of Peire Vidal, a twelfth century troubadour from Provence, France.
ISBN 0-8225-1915-1 (lib. bdg. : alk. paper)
1. Troubadours—Juvenile literature. 2. Peire Vidal, fl. 1200—Juvenile fiction.
[1. Troubadours. 2. Peire Vidal, fl. 1200—Fiction.] I. Bacchin, Giorgio, ill. II. Clift, Dominique. III. Title. IV. Series.
PC3304.P4713   1997
841'.109—dc21   96-38952

Manufactured in the United States of America
1 2 3 4 5 6 – JR – 02 01 00 99 98 97

CONTENTS

Introduction by Series Editors / 6

PART ONE

**The World of a
Medieval Troubadour / 7**

PART TWO

**A Day with Peire Vidal,
a Twelfth-Century Troubadour / 17**

Afterword by Series Editors / 42

Glossary / 43

Pronunciation Guide / 45

Further Reading / 46

Index / 47

About the Author and the Illustrator / 48

INTRODUCTION

Middle Ages and *medieval* are terms that refer to a period in European history. This period, which lasted from roughly A.D. 500 to A.D. 1500, is sandwiched between the Roman Empire and the **Renaissance,** or rebirth of interest in classical Greece and Rome. The ideas that took root during the Renaissance mark the beginning of the modern era of Europe's history.

During the Middle Ages, the lives of the people of Europe were centered around two important factors—the power of the **Roman Catholic Church** and the power of the **landowners.** These two factors shaped European society.

The Catholic Church, in addition to taking care of religious matters, offered opportunities for education, fostered the arts (such as music and sculpture), and paid for massive building projects. People at every level of medieval life held strongly to Christian beliefs, and the decorations on churches were symbols of this faith and devotion.

The landowners—usually noble lords who lived in castles—held power under a governing system known as **feudalism.** Although a lord might owe loyalty to a king, within his own territory, the lord managed agriculture, trade, and industry. He collected taxes, demanded military service, and made judicial decisions.

Most ordinary people, known as **peasants,** lived and worked on the lord's land and had few rights. They tilled his soil, cut his wood, repaired his buildings—in short they did whatever the lord asked of them. In return, the lord used his knights to provide peace and security.

Some common folk, mainly merchants and **artisans,** were residents of towns. By about the eleventh century— the beginning of the **High Middle Ages**—Europe had many towns and several large cities. The first towns had been set up near castles, but as local trade grew, towns also developed along rivers and other commercial routes. Peasants began to leave rural areas to find jobs in towns. Craftworkers, merchants, food vendors, and innkeepers made up the towns' populations. Some peasants farmed their own land outside the towns and provided the townspeople with food.

This story of a medieval **troubadour** takes place during the High Middle Ages in Provence, a region of southern France. Troubadours were respected artists, crafting words into poetry and weaving it with music to convey a message. These poet-musicians wrote about a variety of subjects, but they are perhaps best known for their love songs. Many of these songs—including some by Peire Vidal, the troubadour portrayed in this book—have survived to the present day.

Series Editors

PART ONE

THE WORLD OF A
MEDIEVAL TROUBADOUR

In Provençal, the language of Provence, a *troubadour* is a "finder" or an "inventor." During the Middle Ages, the term was used to describe anyone who wrote or composed anything. Poets often were also musicians who sang their verses. The troubadour tradition began in the Provence region of southern France at the end of the eleventh century. The first troubadours composed their poems in Latin, the language of the Roman Catholic Church.

(Above) *Some troubadours were great travelers, going from one city or feudal* **court** *to another. This poet-musician rides horseback, with his musical instrument slung across his back.*

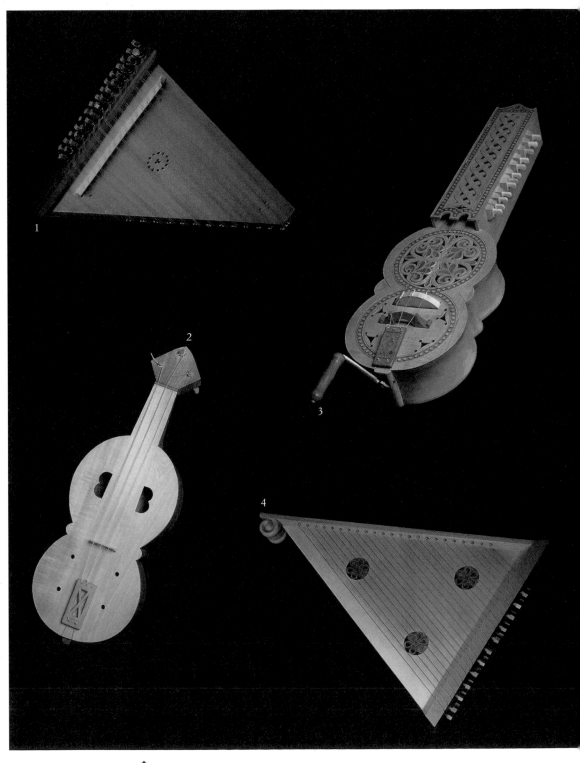

(Right) *Music was deeply rooted in the cultural traditions of the Middle Ages. Among medieval instruments were: 1 and 9, zithers or* **kitharas;** *2, 5, 6 and 7, viols or fiddles, three shaped as a figure eight and one oval; 3, a* **hurdy-gurdy** *with the crank at the bottom and the small keyboard at the top; 4, a* **psaltery,** *similar to a kithara; and 8, a harp.*

But later poet-musicians used local languages, such as Provençal in southern France. Gradually the troubadour form of expression spread throughout France and into neighboring lands. Records from the twelfth and thirteenth centuries name about 460 troubadours. Some, such as Bernard de Ventadour, left complete collections of their works, while many are known only through a few verses.

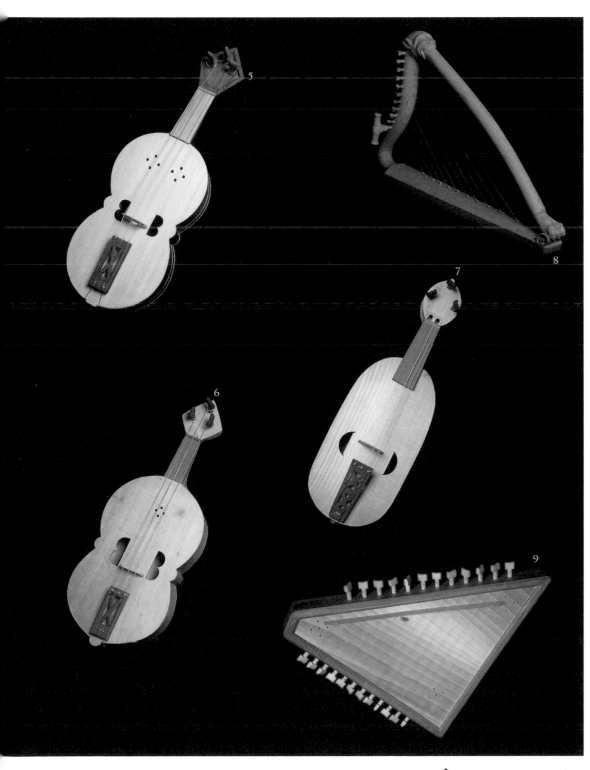

(Above) *Troubadours spread from France to Italy, Germany, and Spain in the twelfth century. They were interested in the new ways of life that developed around the feudal courts. They observed the courtesies a **vassal**, or servant, paid his lord. The troubadours applied this code of conduct to noblewomen. Troubadours composed poems to express love and loyalty to a lady of the court whom they admired from afar. This tradition came to be known as **courtly love.** It kindled a revolution in manners and customs—the beginnings of **romantic love.***

Troubadours created a new kind of poetry based on the way of life around the feudal courts. As part of feudalism, landowners were ranked according to the amount of land and power they held. Even the most powerful lord was considered a vassal. Being a vassal meant a man owed loyalty to an overlord—the lord or king who was immediately above him in rank. A vassal showed loyalty by performing services, including defending his overlord from enemies. In return, overlords gave their vassals land to use. In dealing with overlords, vassals followed a new standard for courtly manners, from which came the modern expression **courtesy.**

An admiration for someone loved from afar inspired many troubadour poems. The poet sang of the love and respect he felt toward his chosen lady, or noblewoman. Yet he also had to accept separa-

(Above) *A miniature, or small painting of great detail, represents the Garden of Eden as a city. The illustration comes from a medieval book called* Liber Floridus. *Cities and castles were among the main centers of cultural and artistic life during the Middle Ages. These communities were small but very lively. In the twelfth century, a true urban renewal took place. The city symbolized the perfection that people believed should be the goal of the human race.* (Right) *Loarre Castle in Spain dates from the eleventh century. As the heart of medieval life, the castle was a safe place where peasants lived under the protection of a feudal lord. Castles also attracted merchants and craftspeople, including architects, painters, and troubadours.*

tion from her, for they could never be united. His songs reflected a mixture of joy when thinking of his lady and suffering from not being with her. One look brought happiness to the poet and led him to great deeds. From this troubadour tradition came the medieval **romances** of the twelfth century, including the legends of Lancelot and Guinevere and of Tristan and Isolde.

Many troubadours, including the renowned Provençal poet-musician Guillaume of Aquitaine, belonged to the **nobility.** But many others were of humble origins. Peire Vidal, who composed his poems between 1180 and 1200, was the son of a **furrier** from the city of Toulouse. His singing was first noticed by Barral des Baux, viscount of Marseilles.

The story that follows describes the stormy life of Peire Vidal, the son of a furrier from Toulouse, in southern France. Workshops selling hides and furs (above) were typical small industries during the Middle Ages. For supplies, the master furrier relied on trustworthy merchants to obtain furs from far and wide. (Left) Because of the social system of the day, the lords in the castles had many servants. As a result, the wealthy could take the time to enjoy the arts. In a society where reading and writing were not widespread, poetry sung to music became a very popular form of entertainment.

(Right) *This map shows a network of roads that led* **pilgrims,** *or religious travelers, to Spain beginning in the ninth century. At that time, a Roman Catholic bishop named Teodomiro claimed he had found the tomb of the apostle Saint James in what is now northwestern Spain. Gradually, Christians from all over western Europe began making* **pilgrimages** *to Santiago, the city that grew up around the tomb. Hospitals, hospices, and religious sites were built along the roads to serve the pilgrims. Trade and social events began taking place in the regions crossed by the roads. Merchants and craftspeople could connect with people from faraway places, spreading new goods and ideas to different regions. With so much activity, these roads were choice routes for troubadours. Les Baux (inset map), the locale of the story that follows, is close to one of the roads leading to Santiago. Catholic monks built three abbeys in the area during the twelfth century. The abbeys of Le Thoronet, Silvacane, and Sénanque housed monks who served pilgrims on their way to Santiago and other holy places.*

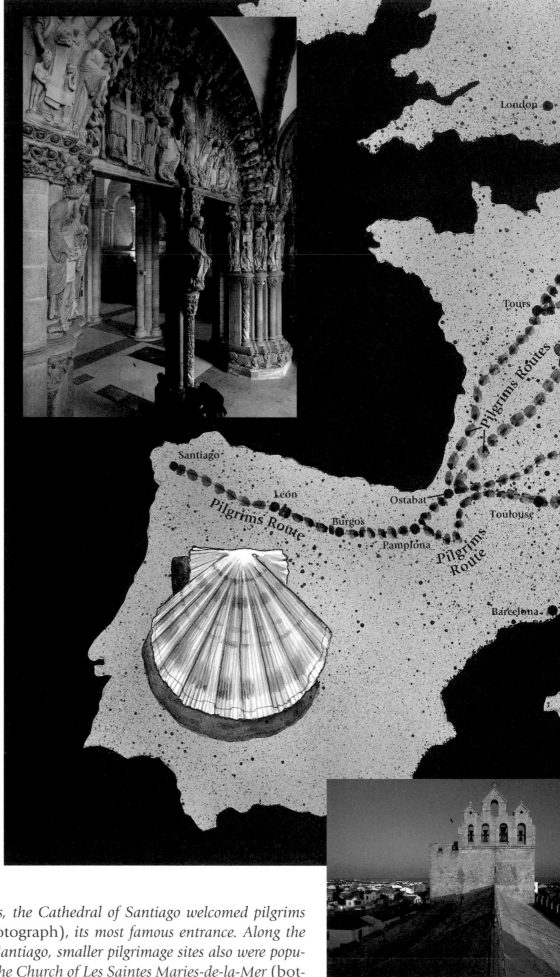

Built above the tomb of Saint James, the Cathedral of Santiago welcomed pilgrims through the Door of Glory (top photograph), its most famous entrance. Along the routes to major pilgrimages such as Santiago, smaller pilgrimage sites also were popular. South of Les Baux, a road led to the Church of Les Saintes Maries-de-la-Mer (bottom photograph). Built in part to honor the patron of **Gypsies,** *the church is the focus of a pilgrimage and festival attended each year by Gypsies from all over Europe.*

Pilgrims who had reached Santiago proclaimed their achievement by wearing a ribbed shell they had collected on nearby Atlantic beaches. Called the shell of Saint James, it was displayed on a pouch or other item of clothing.

Pilgrims Route

Aachen

Paris

Vézelay

Konstanz

Pilgrims Route

Einsiedeln

Geneva

Le Puy

Milan

Venice

Pilgrims Route

Torino

Arles

Pilgrims Route

Signa

MEDITERRANEAN
SEA

Rome

Rhône River

Verdon River

Avignon

Sénanque

Durance R.

Durance River

Les Baux

Silvacane

Rhône River

Arles

Aix-en-Provence

Le Thoronet

Les Saintes
Maries-de-
la-Mer

Marseilles

Provence

During the Middle Ages, fairs were very important events. At first they were linked to religious celebrations and held at favorable seasonal times. Eventually, the fairs provided major opportunities for trade. The events lasted several days. Considerable time and effort went into the organization of the site and of the services that visitors would need. Preparations included booths for exhibits, pens for the animals, and lodgings for travelers to supplement what local inns and hostels could provide. Besides religious celebrations and trade opportunities, fairs were occasions for performances, tournaments, and other cultural entertainments.

The place Peire Vidal loved best was Provence, a region along the Mediterranean Sea in southern France. The castle at Les Baux, where the following story takes place, still attracts a large number of tourists, as do nearby sites such as the church at Les Saintes Maries-de-la-Mer, where Gypsies still go on pilgrimage. Also in the vicinity is a group of abbeys called the "three sisters." All three—Le Thoronet, Sénanque, and Silvacane—date from the twelfth century.

This illustration shows the town of Les Baux as it appeared during the late twelfth century and early thirteenth century. Modern visitors are impressed by its spectacular natural site. Les Baux looks like a gigantic rock ship, its great hull stranded on gentle sandy slopes at the end of a valley. The castle (2) is still a tourist attraction. The adjoining **dungeon** was under construction around 1200. The site's other medieval-era buildings are: the Paravelle Tower (1), the Tower of Bannes (3), the Saracen Tower (4), St. Blaise's Chapel (5), and the mill (6).

The fictional story that follows is based on historical references to a real troubadour named Peire Vidal, who created most of his songs in the late twelfth century. At that time, what is now France was made up of several small principalities. From 1174 to 1393, a powerful family of princes ruled much of Provence from their home base at Les Baux. Peire gained favor at Les Baux, and this recognition helped ensure his success as a troubadour.

Peire described Provence as a region that stretched from the Rhone River eastward to the town of Vence (near Nice). The Mediterranean Sea marked Provence's southern limit, while the Durance River bordered the north. Routes taken by pilgrims crossed the region. These people were traveling to religious shrines. Some, such as Les Saintes Maries-de-la-Mer, lay within Provence. Others were much farther away.

Many travelers were bound for Palestine, the birthplace of the Christian religion on the eastern shores of the Mediterranean Sea. Christians called the area the Holy Land. Since the seventh century, Palestine had been controlled by Arab Muslims, who followed the Islamic religion, which also began in Palestine. For the most part, Arab Muslims continued to allow Christians to visit Palestine. Occasionally, a group of Arab Muslims called the Saracens would invade and loot Christian territory. (The Saracen Tower at Les Baux served as a lookout post for Saracen pirates.) But Christian pilgrims were free to visit sites in the Holy Land until the eleventh century, when Seljuk Turks took over Palestine and stopped Christian pilgrims.

In 1095 the Roman Catholic pope organized the **Crusades** (a series of holy wars) to help regain the Holy Land from the Seljuk Muslims. The Crusades began the following year. Thousands of Europeans went to Palestine. Not everyone joined these military expeditions for religious reasons. Feudal knights from France sought land. Italian merchants hoped to increase trade with the Middle East. Many poor people were trying to get away from the hardships of everyday life. Peire Vidal joined for adventure and to escape dishonor at Les Baux. In the story that follows, he has returned from the Crusades and has just arrived for a fair in his native Provence.

PART TWO

A DAY WITH PEIRE VIDAL, A TWELFTH-CENTURY TROUBADOR

Returning to Provence,
My heartbeat was a song.

This will be the beginning of my next song, thought Peire Vidal, humming as the night gave way to dawn. The troubadour was happy to be back in Provence. Of all the places he had been, this was the country he liked best. He had traveled to many lands since leaving his father's furrier workshop in Toulouse. His father had wanted him to stay and learn how to tan hides of sheep, goats, foxes, and bears. The hides were specially treated to convert them into leather. Then they were lined for overalls and coats that peddlers traded at local fairs. But Peire had had little taste for leather and fur. What he had wanted to do was to see the world. But he still loved coming back to his homeland, with its blue skies and never-ending sunsets. He had said as much in one of his songs:

There is no sweeter home
Than land from Rhone to Vence,
Held by sea and Durance.

The land within this area, on the road to Les Baux, was where he had spent his youth. How many memories! Every turn of the road called back a beautiful moment, sitting under a pure blue sky. In the distance, he could see the castle's Saracen Tower. It had been used as a watchtower to forestall surprises by Saracen pirates hiding out in neighboring mountains.

Thoughts of the Holy Land set Peire humming again. He had been there not such a long time ago. Along with some companions, he had boarded a ship in Genoa, Italy, to join King Richard the Lion-Hearted, who was fighting to rescue the city of Acre. But Peire had not stayed long with the Crusaders. He had gone to the island of Cyprus, where he had married a Greek woman. They had lived happily, but she had died.

Finding himself alone, Peire chose to return to Provence. He could have gone south to Barcelona in Spain, where he had been well received. To this day, they were singing his songs at the court of the king of Aragon in northeastern Spain. Or he could have gone east, where he had been invited, or to the north. Even the Magyars of Hungary beckoned. But the call of Provence had been strongest. And now, the wheel of a windmill turning in the breeze told him he would soon see the Paravelle Tower and then the castle. It was toward this castle that memories were leading him . . . memories of his youth!

As the sun rose in the sky, he saw more people on the road. Two days earlier, **heralds** had announced a tournament at the castle at Les Baux. Peire planned to attend, and many others had the same idea. He had passed a group of pilgrims bound southward to a place called Les Saintes Maries-de-la-Mer. For awhile they had traveled together. Peire had once made the trip to this shrine, which honored an image of the Virgin Mary with black features that showed through her veil. He also came upon two monks traveling northward. They were from the abbey of Le Thoronet. Awhile later Peire was overtaken by a pack of mules and donkeys driven by scrambling stable hands. Merchants on horseback were bringing up the rear. They, too, were going to the tournament and would be setting up their stalls not far from the field of the festivities. Merchants always found it profitable to go where people came together and had fun.

As the sun continued to rise in the sky, Peire saw traveling groups of knights and ladies en route to the tournament. They exchanged merry greetings with one another. But he mused that not one of them could guess his happy thoughts. The one feeling driving him down this road to Les Baux was his eagerness to find his lady again. Would she be there?

Peire instinctively held back his horse, as memories of his youth intruded on his happiness. They were memories he was not ready to share. At the outset of his adventurous life, he had fallen in love with a woman called Loba, or *She-wolf*. To attract attention and to do her honor, he had worn a wolf skin. But three watchdogs had attacked him. Peire had had a hard time defending himself and had finally been rescued by the dogs' shepherd as they were about to strangle him. It had been an embarrassing scene, hardly designed to please Loba.

He had left in a hurry and had gone to Les Baux. He had been there once before, after Barral des Baux had heard him sing in Marseilles and had persuaded the troubadour to come to his castle. This second time he had met his lady, Azalais, the wife of Barral. These had been happy times. Every day he had created new poems and songs. His songs had made Azalais happy, and, when she had looked at him, her eyes had lit up with a flame that had melted his heart. Peire had composed poem after poem to her. He had called her Vierna for springtime, and the name had seemed to please her. Until the day had come when. . . .

Peire felt the need to stop for a moment. His horse was thirsty, and there was a fountain ahead on the side of the road.

While his horse drank, Peire savored a memory that he cherished. One day he had entered the great hall of the castle and had seen Vierna asleep on the cushions of a large armchair. Very softly, he had come near her. He had been so close that he had not been able to resist the temptation to kiss her . . . . It had been an impulsive and reckless thing to do, for he had not heard the stable boy entering the chamber. Vierna's cry on being surprised in her sleep had startled the boy. And right behind him had been Barral himself.

The upshot of the incident had been a long trip—to Spain, the Holy Land, and Cyprus.

But on this day, he was in Provence again, and each step brought him closer to his Lady Vierna, Azalais. Peire got back on his horse and continued on his way. He decided he would not actually approach her. Yet she was bound to hear him and would surely recognize his singing. Another poem came to mind, composed a long time ago by the Provençal troubadour, Guillaume of Aquitaine. It began with, "The sweetness of new times." There was one stanza that Peire thought very beautiful:

So is it with our love
As with the hawthorn branch
That trembles on the tree
At night, in rain, and frost,
Until dawn when the sun
Smiles on leaves and greenery.

But this was not the poem he planned to sing. It would be one of his own, one he felt wouldn't be long taking wing.

At midmorning, as Peire came closer to the hill of Les Baux, the noise ahead pulled him out of his reverie. The narrow streets were jammed with people, some going up and others coming down. There were animals with heavy loads, a herald crying news no one could possibly hear, two merchants trading insults, the usual holiday crowd, water carriers, housewives with baskets. Peire found it unbelievably hard to make any headway. Yet, no matter what, he had to reach the yard of the castle. Lurching from lane to lane, the troubadour moved forward, then lost ground, while children ran wild cutting in and out of the moving mass of people. Peire realized he should imitate them. He was close to St. Blaise's Chapel and the inn next to it. He would stop there, put his horse in the stable, and continue on foot. It was only a short walk to the castle and to the open field where the tournament would take place.

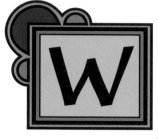

When Peire arrived at the castle around noon, he barely recognized the place. At the base of some construction he had never seen were barricades, and stands had been put up for the tournament. He thought the new construction must be the dungeon that the lord of the castle had planned to build. To his right, he recognized the Tower of Bannes, where people's homes were carved out of the rock.

But his mind was not on the scenery. He moved toward the fence marking the field where the tournament would take place. He positioned himself right in front of the stands decorated with draperies and foliage, where some noblewomen had already taken seats. From where he stood, he had a view of the whole scene. The knights taking part in the tournament had already gathered on the field. They were dressing for combat, putting on suits of armor with the help of their **squires.** The knights' pennants and flags with coats of arms fluttered in the breeze. Peire did not want to miss any part of the action. He folded his coat and sat waiting. Feeling hungry, he bit into a piece of bread stuffed with cheese that he had brought for lunch.

Within an hour, the herald's trumpet sounded. The tournament was beginning. Two knights sprang up and took positions at opposite sides of the field. They made fantastic figures. Each knight and horse was dressed in colorful garments bearing the coat of arms of the lord they served. The two knights moved toward one another for the first pass in the bout. Their horses were excited by the cries of the crowd. The combatants rode lance in hand and crossed one another. One of the knights was thrown off balance when his opponent's solid blow hit his shield. But he wrenched himself back into the saddle and prepared for the next pass. In the stands, one of the noblewomen stood up waving a silvery veil—the prize that would reward the winner.

Peire began taking an interest in the galloping knights. He took his coat and stood up, leaning against the fence for a better view of the action.

The bouts continued. One knight was brutally unhorsed. Another one limped away, knocked out of the contest by a blow that he had barely managed to deflect with his shield. The losers' horses were prizes for the winners. After the encounters between pairs of knights were over, the action became more intense and exciting. The main tournament event began, as two rows of knights faced each other in combat.

In the stands, the noblewomen were very excited, too. Each had a champion she hoped would triumph.

P eire suddenly lost all interest in the action and was indifferent to the great heat of the late afternoon. In one of the decorated compartments stood his lady. It was Azalais, or Vierna, the symbol of spring. She was still very beautiful, with a long violet dress with a bright sheen. On her arm she wore a ruby red scarf. Her beautiful brown hair was covered with a golden net. Peire, his mind on his past love, saw his lady as young and beautiful as she had ever been. She was now waving her scarf and clapping her hands at the exploits of one of the knights. He seemed certain to win the prize. It was a beautiful bird, a hunting bird—a trained falcon with a hood. As the cheers and enthusiasm grew more intense, the bird remained absolutely motionless on a perch. With carefully gloved hands, a squire displayed the falcon to the crowd. The gloves protected the squire from the bird's talons (claws).

The hours passed quickly. It was soon evening. After the knights' exploits, a sudden calm fell on the field. A singer moved forward with a kithara. After a few notes, the crowd hushed and turned its attention to the music. The soothing sounds of the stringed instrument were a welcome change after the clash of arms and the cheering. Peire listened along with the crowd. But he never stopped humming in his mind the song he had been thinking about since he set out on his trip to Les Baux. In this joyous atmosphere and in view of his lady, he felt he could improvise one verse after another.

The singer, who certainly had talent, deserved the strong support he got from the crowd. But Peire felt he could do better. At the end of the song, the entertainers took over the jousting field. One of them was doing somersaults and making funny faces on the back of an ox. Another was juggling colored balls. Still another was throwing little hoops in the air with a stick and retrieving them with elegance. There were also many acrobats. People in the stands cheered and tossed coins to them. While the performers saluted the crowd, Peire impulsively jumped the fence into the field.

Peire had no instrument with him. But his strong voice attracted the attention of the crowd, which began to listen in silence. Peire sang a long poem composed in his mind in praise of Provence and of his lady.

With every sigh, I breathe
The sweet air of Provence.
The words of praise I hear
Are smiles that rejoice me:
One word should be hundreds
So much pleasure they give.

There is no sweeter home
Than land from Rhone to Vence,
Held by sea and Durance.
Where joy and light are bright,
Among noble people
I left my loving heart
To her whose smile is balm.

Peire turned toward the stands, boldly looking toward Lady Vierna, who was sitting upright in her armchair, obviously moved. Encouraged by the silence of the listening crowd, he continued:

Can one admonish fate
When he remembers her?
All joy begins with her,
And he who praises her

Does not lie as he says,
More gracious is not seen,
More lovely ever born.

And whatever I do
Or speak begins with her,
She who bestowed the power
Of gladness and knowledge.
Whatever I have done,
Her grace has inspired me.
It gave me happiness.

By the time Peire concluded his song, the sun had set. He made his way through the crowd and jumped once more over the fence. He paid no attention to the appreciative looks he received or to the people who turned to greet him. In her seat in the stands, Lady Vierna called a squire, whispered a few things in his ear, and entrusted him with her ruby red scarf. Perhaps Peire saw the scene, but he was moved so deeply that he continued through the crowd to the inn where he had left his horse.

When the squire arrived with the scarf, Peire was already gone, guiding his horse down the little paths from the hill of Les Baux. But the troubadour was happy. His lady had recognized him from his song. In a few verses, he was able to remind her of his love. He did not need anything more on this day, which he would always remember as a happy one. He wanted to continue his life as a troubadour, wandering from castle to castle, carrying in his heart the image of Lady Vierna, the love of his youth, the one who would ever be his lady.

AFTERWORD

From roughly 1100 to 1300, the troubadour tradition flourished, with Provence at its heart. As this form of expression passed to other lands, it left a lasting mark on them as well. Troubadour poetry influenced literature in Spain, Germany, and especially Italy. Poets in these places began writing literature in their native language instead of in Latin. And they applied the codes of courtly love to their poems.

Beginning in the 1300s, Dante and other great Italian writers carried the troubadour tradition to a new level in which the honored lady lives forever. Love became a major theme in European literature. Long after the feudal courts died out in Provence, courtly behavior lived on to guide relations between men and women.

The troubadours spoke not only to women. Poets carefully crafted words to have several layers of meaning and to speak to the various social classes in a court audience. Often poems were addressed to a vague person. In so doing, troubadours flattered not only the women of a court but also lords, vassals, and a growing population of freemen (the sons of peasants whom noble lords could not afford to keep). By speaking to so many different groups, troubadours imparted a sense of equality and freedom that was otherwise unheard of in feudal society. Some poems were openly political. Some even criticized the power of the Church.

As the Middle Ages drew to a close, troubadours were not the only people to criticize the power of the Church or the rigid social structure of feudal society. Gradually, society grew freer as increased trade improved the economy and fostered the growth of cities. People began to have some choice in how they made a living. They no longer depended on an overlord for food and protection. As both feudal lords and the Church lost power, social thought shifted toward the importance of individuals. A movement called humanism viewed all people as good and deserving of admiration.

While troubadours may not have been the first to express humanist ideas, they helped awaken medieval society to these ideals. Humanism, including a rejection of rule by the few, has remained popular. In fact, the movement had a strong impact on governments that were set up in France and the United States in later centuries.

Glossary

artisan: A person skilled at a certain craft.

court: The residence of a lord or other ruler. The word also applies to the group of people who are at the ruler's service. A court was originally the open space—the courtyard—that the residence enclosed.

courtesy: In the Middle Ages, courtesy referred to behavior befitting a feudal court. It included courtly elegance, polite manners, and respect for the position and feelings of others. We still use the term to refer to good manners.

courtly love: The admiration from afar of a lady of a feudal court.

Crusade: Any of the wars that Christians from Europe fought from the eleventh to the thirteenth centuries to capture the Holy Land from the Muslims.

dungeon: A tower that is the highest and best fortified part of a medieval castle where residents could be safe in case of attack. After the Middle Ages, dungeons served as prisons and were usually underground and dark.

feudalism: The land-based governing system that operated in Europe from the ninth to about the fifteenth centuries.

furrier: Someone who prepares furs for clothing. The pelts are cleaned and softened, then trimmed and sewn together to make garments.

Gypsy: A member of a wandering people with dark skin and black hair, found throughout the world. They are thought to have come originally from India.

herald: In the Middle Ages, a person who publicly announced news of common interest to a community and who carried messages for a lord or king.

hurdy-gurdy: A stringed instrument sounded by turning a crank that spins a metal wheel against a set of strings. A small keyboard allows musicians to change pitch and play songs.

kithara: An ancient stringed instrument of the harp family with a sound box beneath the strings.

landowner: Under the feudal system, the owner of agricultural land who had power over every aspect of life on the property and made up Europe's ruling class for 400 years. In addition to managing their estates, feudal landowners could tax farmers, demand military service, arrange marriages, and impose judicial decisions.

Middle Ages: A period of European history that lasted from roughly A.D. 500 to A.D. 1500. The greatest achievements of the period, known as the **High Middle Ages,** came in the eleventh and twelfth centuries.

nobility: The small, privileged class of people who hold land and power. The nobility, or nobles, usually have titles such as duke, count, or earl.

peasant: A person who tills the soil on land that usually belongs to someone else.

pilgrimage: A long religious journey to a holy place or shrine. People who go on pilgrimages are called **pilgrims.**

psaltery: An early musical instrument with strings stretched over a soundboard in the shape of a triangle. Later, with the addition of a keyboard, it developed into the harpsichord and, eventually, the piano.

Renaissance: A period of European history that followed the Middle Ages and blended into the modern era. Lasting from the fourteenth to the seventeenth centuries, the Renaissance took its name from the French word for "rebirth." The period is known for a rebirth of interest in the arts, literature, and learning of classical Roman civilization.

Roman Catholic Church: A Christian re-ligious organization that was founded in the late Roman Empire. After the empire's fall in the fifth century A.D., chaos followed. The Catholic Church became the main source of leadership, political power, and education until the feudal system evolved in the ninth century.

romance: A medieval tale based on legend, courtly love, and adventure. The word is now also used to describe a love story in general. These stories were originally told in Romance languages (the languages of the Roman Empire). The spirit of love, devotion, and courtesy between a knight and lady portrayed in medieval romances came to be called **romantic love.**

squire: A knight's servant. During the Middle Ages, young men who wanted to become knights would first become squires to learn the skills of knighthood from the knight they served. Usually only men of noble birth could afford to be knights, since armor and a war horse were expensive.

troubadour: A poet-musician of the late Middle Ages who wrote and sang poems about love and knighthood. Troubadours flourished in southern France during the twelfth and thirteenth centuries.

vassal: A person in the feudal system who held land in return for providing military and other help to an overlord.

Pronunciation Guide

Azalais	ahz-ah-LAY
Bannes	BAHN
Barral des Baux	bahr-AHL day BOH
Bernard de Ventadour	behr-NAHR duh VAHN-tuh-dor
Durance	doo-RAHNS
feudalism	FYOO-duhl-ih-zuhm
Guillaume of Aquitaine	gee-YOHM uhv AH-kwuh-tayn
kithara	KIH-thuh-ruh
Le Thoronet	luh toh-roh-NAY
Les Baux	LAY BOH
Les Saintes Maries-de-la-Mer	lay sant mah-ree–duh–lah–MEHR
Marseilles	mahr-SAY
medieval	mee-DEE-vuhl
Peire Vidal	PEHR vee-DAHL
Provençal	proh-vahn-SAHL
Provence	proh-VAHNS
psaltery	SAHL-tuh-ree
Renaissance	REH-nuh-sahns
Sénanque	say-NAHNK
Silvacane	sihl-vah-KAHN
Toulouse	tuh-LOOZ
troubadour	TROO-buh-dohr
Vence	VAHNS
Vierna	vee-EHR-nah
viol	VY-ohl

FURTHER READING LIST

Barber, Nicola, and Mure, Mary. *The World of Music.* Parsippany, NJ: Silver Burdett, 1996.

Corbishley, Mike. *Cultural Atlas for Young People: The Middle Ages.* New York: Facts On File, 1990.

France in Pictures. Minneapolis: Lerner Publications Company, Geography Department, 1991.

Ganeri, Anita. *France and the French.* New York: Gloucester Press, 1993.

Gravett, Christopher. *Eyewitness Books: Castle.* New York: Alfred A. Knopf, 1994.

Howarth, Sarah. *Medieval People.* Brookfield, CT: The Millbrook Press, 1992.

Howarth, Sarah. *See Through History: The Middle Ages.* New York: Viking, 1993.

Ingman, Nicholas. *The Story of Music.* New York: Taplinger Publishing Company, 1976.

Langley, Andrew. *Eyewitness Books: Medieval Life.* New York: Alfred A. Knopf, 1996.

Oakes, Catherine. *Exploring the Past: The Middle Ages.* San Diego: Harcourt Brace Jovanovich, 1989.

Weisberg, Barbara. *The Big Golden Book of Knights and Castles.* Racine, WI: Western Publishing Company, Inc., 1993.

INDEX

abbeys, 12, 14, 22
Azalais. *See* Vierna

Baux, Barral des, 11, 24, 26

castle, 14, 15, 18, 20, 22, 24–31
Cathedral of Santiago, 12
Christian beliefs, 6, 12, 16
conduct, codes of, 9, 42. *See also* courtesy
courtesy, 10
courtly love, 9, 42
craftspeople, 6, 10, 12
Crusades, 16, 20
Cyprus, 20, 26

Durance River, 16, 18, 38

fairs, 14, 18. *See also* tournaments
feudal courts, 8, 9, 10, 42
feudalism, 6, 10, 42
France, 9, 11, 16. *See also* Provence
furrier, 11, 18

Guillaume of Aquitaine, 11, 26
Gypsies, 12, 14

Holy Land, 16, 20, 26
humanism, 42
instruments, musical, 8–9, 36, 42

knights, 6, 16, 22, 30–35, 36

landowners, 6, 10
language, 9, 42. *See also* Provençal
Les Baux, 12, 14, 15, 16, 18, 24. *See also* castle

Les Saintes Maries-de-la-Mer, 12, 14, 16, 22
Le Thoronet, 12, 14, 22
Liber Floridus, 10
Loarre Castle, 10
Loba, 24
lords, noble, 6, 10, 11, 32, 42
love, 9, 10–11, 24, 42. *See also* troubadours, love songs of

manners. *See* courtesy
map, 12–13
Marseilles, 11, 24
Mediterranean Sea, 14, 16
merchants, 6, 10, 11, 12, 16, 22
Middle Ages: close of, 42; definition of, 6
monks, 12, 22
music, 6, 8, 9. *See also* instruments, musical; troubadours
Muslims, 16

noblewomen, 9, 10, 30, 32, 33, 42

Palestine, 16
Paravelle Tower, 15, 20
peasants, 6, 10
pilgrimages, 12, 14
pilgrims, 12, 13, 16, 22
Provençal, 9, 11, 24, 26
Provence, 6, 9, 14, 16, 18, 20, 26, 38, 42

religion, 14. *See also* Christian beliefs; Muslims
Renaissance, 6
Rhone River, 16, 18, 38
Richard the Lion-Hearted, King, 20

Roman Catholic Church, 6, 9, 12, 16, 42
Roman Empire, 6
romantic love, 9, 11

St. Blaise's Chapel, 15, 28
Saint James: shell of, 13; tomb of, 12
Santiago, 12, 13
Saracen pirates, 16, 18
Saracen Tower, 15, 16, 18
songs. *See* troubadours, love songs of
Spain, 10, 12, 20, 26

Teodomiro, 12
Toulouse, 11, 18
tourism, 14, 15
tournaments, 14, 28, 30–40
Tower of Bannes, 15, 30
trade, 6, 12, 14, 16, 42
troubadours: background of, 11; definition of, 6, 9; language of, 9; love songs of, 6, 9, 10–11, 16, 24, 26, 36, 38, 40; travels of, 8, 12, 18

vassals, 9, 10, 42
Vence, 16, 18, 38
Ventadour, Bernard de, 9
Vidal, Peire, 6, 11, 14, 16, 18–41
Vierna, 24–27, 34, 38–40

women. *See* noblewomen

About the
Author and the Illustrator

Régine Pernoud, an internationally known expert on life in the Middle Ages, studied at L'Ecole de Chartres and L'Ecole du Louvre before becoming curator successively of the Museum of Reims in Reims, the Museum of the History of France at the National Archives in Paris, and the Joan of Arc Center in Orléans. A resident of Paris, Ms. Pernoud is the author of more than 40 scholarly works translated into many languages.

Giorgio Bacchin, a native of Milan, Italy, studied the graphic arts in his hometown. After years of freelance graphic design, Mr. Bacchin has completely devoted himself to book illustration. His works have appeared in educational and trade publications.